The Karate Kid Part II

A novelization for young readers by B.B. Hiller.
Based on the motion picture written by Robert Mark Kamen.
Based on characters created by Robert Mark Kamen.

SCHOLASTIC INC.
New York Toronto London Auckland Sydney

The
Karate Kid II
Part II

COLUMBIA PICTURES Presents
A JERRY WEINTRAUB PRODUCTION A JOHN G. AVILDSEN FILM
RALPH MACCHIO NORIYUKI "PAT" MORITA
THE KARATE KID
PART II
Music by BILL CONTI Music Supervisor BROOKS ARTHUR Production Designed by WILLIAM J. CASSIDY
Director of Photography JAMES CRABE Executive Producer R.J. LOUIS Written by ROBERT MARK KAMEN
Based on Characters Created by ROBERT MARK KAMEN Produced by JERRY WEINTRAUB
DOLBY STEREO READ THE SCHOLASTIC BOOK Directed by JOHN G. AVILDSEN

ISBN 0-590-40291-9

12 11 10 9 8 7 6 5 4 3 2   6 7 8 9/8 0 1/9

Printed in the U.S.A.   28

for Andy

1

Everything was going wrong for Daniel LaRusso.

He should have been happy. The school year was over. Summer was here. He'd even gone to the prom the night before and stayed up all night. But Daniel was not happy.

He needed to talk to a friend. And when things looked glum for Daniel, there was one friend he knew he'd rather be with than anyone else — Mr. Miyagi.

He walked up to Mr. Miyagi's house, and Mr. Miyagi opened the door.

"Must have been some dance!" Mr. Miyagi teased, looking at Daniel's rumpled suit and the crushed flower in his lapel. Then he saw that Daniel wasn't in a mood to be teased. "What happened?" he asked.

"What *didn't* happen is more like it. First my girl friend was driving my car and dented the fender. Then, she told me she didn't want to be my girl friend anymore."

Daniel's feelings were hurt. Mr. Miyagi tried to comfort him.

"Things could be worse."

"They are," Daniel told him. "Last night my mom told me we have to move to Fresno for the summer while she goes to school."

Mr. Miyagi didn't seem to hear Daniel. He walked out of the house to the driveway where Daniel had parked his car. Then he got down on his hands and knees to look at the dent in the fender.

"Think you can fix it?" Daniel asked.

In answer, Mr. Miyagi used his incredible karate skills to chop firmly at the fender with his hand. The dent popped out and suddenly the fender was back exactly the way it had been before it was dented. Daniel shook his head in awe.

"Come," Mr. Miyagi invited. "I have just the thing to make you feel better."

"What? Poison?" Daniel asked. He was sure nothing *could* make him feel better. He followed Mr. Miyagi around to the back of his house.

Daniel wondered what was in store for him. Mr. Miyagi had a way of surprising Daniel — and everyone else. He was an old man, in his early sixties. He'd been born in Okinawa, near Japan, where his father had trained him to be an expert in karate. In turn, Mr. Miyagi had taught Daniel karate. He was such a good teacher that within three months of the day he started training, Daniel had become the Champion of the All-Valley Under Eighteen Karate Tournament.

But Mr. Miyagi's teaching methods were a little unusual. It had taken Daniel a long time to realize that the "chores" Mr. Miyagi had given him — painting, waxing, sanding — were really part of his lessons. The method may have been unusual, but it worked.

As they came into the garden, Daniel saw that Mr. Miyagi was building an addition on his house. The boards made a skeleton. Now it only needed siding and a roof. Mr. Miyagi picked up two hammers and put one into Daniel's hand.

"How come every time I have problems, you have work for me to do?" Daniel asked, a smile on his face.

Mr. Miyagi shrugged. "Now watch," he told Daniel.

While Daniel watched, Mr. Miyagi hammered a nail all the way into the wood with one blow. "Now you try it," he said, moving aside so Daniel could try. "Remember: Concentrate. Focus."

Daniel tried, but it didn't work. First the nail bent, and then it clattered to the ground.

"I can't," he excused himself. He couldn't focus his attention on the job. He dropped the hammer on the deck.

Mr. Miyagi took Daniel's hands in his and pressed them together in front of him. He looked as if he were going to pray.

"When you fear you are losing focus, always return to basic of life."

"Praying?" Daniel asked, surprised.

"Breathing," Mr. Miyagi told him. Daniel understood. In his karate studies, he had learned that his breath was the center of himself. By breathing properly and timing his movements with his breathing, he could focus. Now, Mr. Miyagi made him reach high above his head, while Daniel breathed out. Then, as Daniel breathed in, Mr. Miyagi brought Daniel's hands back to the prayer position. They repeated the exercise, this time reaching forward, then back.

"Out . . . in . . . out . . . in . . ." Mr. Miyagi reminded him. Then Daniel continued on his own.

"How do you feel?" Mr. Miyagi asked when Daniel was done.

"Better," he told him. "Focused." Daniel reached for the hammer again. This time, he tapped the nail to set it into the wood. Then he drew back his hand and with one swift bang of the hammer, drove the whole nail into the wood.

Being focused made it seem that things weren't so bad after all.

2

The steady tap-*thunk!* of the nails going in took Daniel's mind off his problems.

"Iced-tea, Daniel-san?" Mr. Miyagi asked. He called Daniel "Daniel-san," because in Okinawa, where he had been born, it was respectful to put *san* after a person's name — just as it was respectful for Daniel to call him *Mr.* Miyagi.

"Iced tea would be great," Daniel agreed.

While Mr. Miyagi was in the house making the tea, it occurred to Daniel that he'd been working very hard on an addition to the house, but he didn't know what it was for.

"Say, Mr. Miyagi!" he called into the house. "What am I building out here, anyway?" he asked.

"Guest room."

That was odd. It was a very small house to have a guest room. It didn't even have a living room.

"You expecting company?"

"Expecting a refugee," Mr. Miyagi told him.

"From where?" Daniel asked.

"Fresno," Mr. Miyagi said.

Fresno? That could only mean one thing. Daniel was too excited to speak. Mr. Miyagi appeared with the iced tea.

"Miyagi talked to your mother last night, too," he told Daniel.

"She said I could stay *here*?" Mr. Miyagi's answer was a nod. "That's great, Mr. Miyagi. You've saved my life again. Thanks."

"Welcome."

Daniel couldn't believe his good luck. Only an hour ago, his car was dented and he was going to have to move to Fresno. Now Mr. Miyagi had solved both of those problems. As for the third problem he had — his girl friend dumping him — well, Daniel figured that there must be some other wonderful girl for him somewhere. For now, two out of three problems solved were enough.

Together, they drank the cool tea. It tasted very good on the hot day. Soon, they went to work on the roof. Then there was an interruption.

"Mr. Miyagi! Are you back there?" It was an unfamiliar voice. The gate to the garden banged open and the postman came in. "Are you Mr. Miyagi?" he asked.

"Yes," Mr. Miyagi answered, stepping down the ladder.

The postman held out a letter. "Special delivery from Okinawa," he told him.

Daniel knew that Mr. Miyagi had left Okinawa forty-five years before, but he didn't think that he had kept in touch with anyone there. He could tell, looking at Mr. Miyagi's face, that his friend was worried. Daniel stepped down the ladder to be near him, but Mr. Miyagi took his letter to a corner of the garden to read it by himself. The postman left.

Daniel waited and watched while Mr. Miyagi read the letter and read it again. Mr. Miyagi looked up at him.

"My father is very sick," he explained.

"I didn't know he was still alive," Daniel said, surprised.

"Neither did I," Mr. Miyagi answered.

3

After the arrival of the special-delivery letter, things started happening very quickly.

Of course, Mr. Miyagi had to go to Okinawa to be with his father. Daniel would go to Fresno with his mother, after all.

First, Mr. Miyagi got his airline ticket, and then he got a passport. Daniel helped him pack his suitcase.

Daniel wished there were something else he could do to help Mr. Miyagi. The old man had helped him when he'd been in trouble. Now Daniel wanted to return the favor, but it was hard to think what would be useful.

Daniel and Mr. Miyagi talked while they packed the suitcase. It was odd now to think of Mr. Miyagi returning to Okinawa. It had been a long time since he'd been there. Daniel wanted to know what it had been like.

"How old were you when you left Okinawa?"

9

"Same age as you. Sixteen."

"Why did you leave?" Daniel asked, hoping he wasn't being too nosy, but he was curious. Mr. Miyagi seemed glad to talk. It was almost as if Okinawa had become unreal in his own mind. Talking about it seemed to bring it back to life.

"I fell in love with a girl," Mr. Miyagi explained.

That didn't seem to Daniel like a reason to leave someplace. It sounded more like a reason to *stay.* "So?"

"It was arranged by her parents for her to marry someone else."

"You knew the guy?"

"*Hai,*" Mr. Miyagi answered with the Japanese word for *yes.* "He was my best friend."

Now *that* sounded like a reason to leave someplace.

Mr. Miyagi handed Daniel two very old photographs, yellowed and tattered at the edges. One was of a beautiful young girl, dressed in traditional Japanese clothes. The other was of a handsome young man in a karate outfit, poised to attack. He looked so strong that Daniel thought he could almost jump out of the photograph.

"What's her name?" Daniel asked.

"Yukie. Same woman who wrote me special-delivery letter."

"She's beautiful," Daniel told him.

"*Hai,*" Mr. Miyagi agreed.

11

"And this is your friend?" Daniel asked, looking at the fierce young man.

"Sato," Mr. Miyagi supplied the name. "He challenged me to a fight when he found out about Yukie and me."

"Why?" Daniel asked.

"To save his honor."

"And you *lost*?" Daniel couldn't believe that.

"No." Mr. Miyagi shook his head. "I didn't fight. I left Okinawa forever the next day."

"But you loved her, and she loved you?"

"*Hai.*"

"So how could you leave?" Daniel asked, astonished. This didn't sound like the man he knew.

"Miyagi not believe in fighting."

"But — "

"Never let your heart rule your head, Daniel-san. Even if you win, you lose." Daniel would have to think about that.

"Did they get married?" Daniel asked.

Mr. Miyagi shrugged. "I don't know for sure, but his family was richest in village. Hers was poorest. It was a good arrangement."

"Then he shouldn't be angry about his honor anymore. It was forty-five years ago."

Mr. Miyagi put his slippers in his suitcase. "In Okinawa, honor has no time limit."

That was too much for Daniel. "You've got to

be kidding!" he said, handing the photographs back to Mr. Miyagi.

"Not kidding."

Daniel had a sinking feeling about Mr. Miyagi's trip to Okinawa. At first, it had seemed like the journey would be a sad one because of Mr. Miyagi's father's illness. Now Daniel knew that was only part of what would make the visit hard for his friend. Suddenly Daniel realized he might be the only one who could help make the trip easier for Mr. Miyagi. He had a plan, but he'd have to hurry.

"I've got to go home now," he told the old man. "I'll come back to say good-bye tomorrow."

"Thank you, Daniel-san. I'm sorry things didn't work out for us this summer."

"Me, too," Daniel said. "But maybe they still will."

Mr. Miyagi looked at him, surprised. But before he could say anything, Daniel was gone.

Daniel rushed out of Mr. Miyagi's house. There was a lot he had to do, and little time to do it.

4

A steady stream of people, speaking rapidly among themselves in Japanese, brushed past Daniel and Mr. Miyagi. Daniel could hardly believe it. He was in Okinawa.

It had taken all of his powers of persuasion to get his mother to agree to let him go. Finally, she'd said yes. She knew that he could learn a lot from a summer in Okinawa. But after his mother had agreed, he'd had to convince Mr. Miyagi to take him. That had been tough. In the end, though, Mr. Miyagi had understood that Daniel wanted to be helpful. Daniel was glad to be with his friend.

Okinawa was different from anything Daniel could have imagined. It was a small island — not much bigger than New York City (though with many fewer people). It was now part of Japan, but had been ruled by the United States for thirty years after the second world war. There were still a lot of U.S. military bases on the island, so there were a lot of American men and women there.

Daniel and Mr. Miyagi carried their suitcases through the airport. Daniel stared at the new sights. Because there were so many Americans on Okinawa, many things seemed very familiar. There were posters advertising Coca-Cola and even McDonald's. There were also a lot of signs in Japanese that Daniel didn't understand at all. Many of the people wore American-style clothes. Many others were wearing traditional Japanese clothes. It looked like an odd mixture to Daniel, but nobody else seemed to notice or care.

Suddenly, Daniel saw a familiar face on one of the advertising posters. It was Sato! He was older than in the picture Mr. Miyagi had showed him, but Daniel recognized him right away.

"Look, Mr. Miyagi!" Daniel tugged at his friend's sleeve. "Isn't that him?"

Mr. Miyagi looked at the ad. It showed a picture of Sato in a karate outfit. He was chopping through twelve pieces of wood with his bare hand. The sign said:

LEARN KARATE FROM MASTER SATO
OFFICIAL TEACHER FOR THE U.S. MILITARY
PROVEN IN COMBAT

"*Hai,*" Mr. Miyagi said to Daniel. "That's him."

"Can you break wood like that?" Daniel asked.

15

Mr. Miyagi sniffed in disgust. "Don't know," he answered. "Never been attacked by a tree!" Mr. Miyagi had a funny way of looking at things. Daniel laughed.

Together, they walked out of the airport to the taxi stand. Before they got into a taxi, though, a young man about Daniel's age came up to them.

"Are you Miyagi-san?" he asked politely. When Mr. Miyagi nodded, he spoke again. "It is a great honor to meet you. Yukie-san could not come to the airport. I am Chozen Toguchi." He showed them to a big car, and before they knew what was happening, Chozen put their luggage in the trunk. Still surprised, they climbed into the backseat of the car, and Chozen sat in the front with the driver.

Daniel gazed out the window at Okinawa as they drove.

Mr. Miyagi, however, was watching the road carefully. When the car took an unexpected turn, he tapped on the partition that separated them from Chozen and the driver.

"Isn't the village that way?" Mr. Miyagi asked.

"Some things have changed since you left, Miyagi-san," the driver, Toshio, answered.

"And some things have not," Chozen said ominously.

Suddenly, Daniel was worried. What was Chozen telling them?

5

The next thing Daniel knew, the car turned to enter an airplane hangar. They drove into the big building and stopped. Chozen and Toshio stepped out and opened the doors for Daniel and Mr. Miyagi. They got out from the backseat and stood nervously. Chozen and Toshio removed their luggage from the trunk.

In a few seconds, there was the sound of approaching footsteps.

"Uncle," Chozen said.

A large figure emerged from the shadows and stood near Chozen.

"Sato-san," Mr. Miyagi said.

"So, coward, you have returned!" Sato said in a chilly tone.

"To see my father before he dies," Mr. Miyagi explained.

"And to finish our little unfinished business?" Sato asked.

"I will not fight," Mr. Miyagi told him.

"Then you will die as you have lived — a coward. See your father. Then see me."

With that, Sato turned and got into the backseat of the car. Chozen and Toshio returned to the front seat. Three doors slammed. The engine sparked to life and the car squealed out of the hangar. Mr. Miyagi and Daniel stood alone with their suitcases. Daniel was stunned by what had happened so far in Okinawa. If this was how their visit started, Daniel wondered what would come next.

Mr. Miyagi brought him to his senses, though.

"Come, Daniel-san," he said. "We must find a taxi."

Daniel hoped the taxi would be safer than Sato's car had been.

6

The taxi left Daniel and Mr. Miyagi in front of a small house in the village of Tome. Mr. Miyagi looked at the house carefully. Daniel could see that he was trying to remember what it had looked like when it had been his home so many years ago.

Mr. Miyagi knocked at the door. A girl about Daniel's age opened it and welcomed them. Her name was Kumiko. She helped them with their luggage.

"Yukie is with your father," Kumiko explained, pointing to a room at the rear of the house. Mr. Miyagi slid the door open and entered the room. Daniel and Kumiko followed him.

In the room, Mr. Miyagi's father lay sleeping on a mat on the floor. His breath was shallow and uneven. Yukie kneeled next to him, ready to help him in any way. When the door opened, she looked up. Daniel recognized her right away as the woman

in Mr. Miyagi's photograph. When she saw Mr. Miyagi, she smiled. He smiled at her, too. Then he kneeled on the other side of his father's bed.

"How is he?" he asked.

Yukie looked at him sadly and Mr. Miyagi knew that his father would not live for long. He was very glad that he had come to see him a final time. He held his father's hand.

Just then, Mr. Miyagi's father's eyes fluttered open. He strained to focus, not believing what his eyes told him. He blinked and then looked again. Then he spoke in Japanese.

"What did he say?" Daniel asked Kumiko, who stood next to him.

"He said, 'If I am dreaming, let me never awake. If I am awake, let me never sleep.' "

Daniel, Kumiko, and Yukie left the two men alone.

Kumiko and Daniel talked while she showed him around the little house and helped him unpack the suitcases. Daniel learned that Kumiko was Yukie's niece, not her daughter, for Yukie had never married. Daniel understood that that meant Sato had never married, either. No wonder Sato was still so angry with Mr. Miyagi.

Daniel wondered if Mr. Miyagi might not have been better off if Yukie had never sent the special-delivery letter.

7

The next day, while Mr. Miyagi's father was resting, Mr. Miyagi showed Daniel the family *dojo* — karate gym. Daniel could hardly believe that the house had its own *dojo*, but there it was. This was the very place where his karate master, Mr. Miyagi, had studied.

Daniel loved the *dojo* immediately. He liked the wide open work space, covered with straw mats for protection. He also liked the collection of weapons in a cabinet along one wall. He could see that, in Okinawa, karate was more than a sport. It could be used in life-and-death fights!

On the wall opposite the cabinet was Daniel's favorite part of the *dojo*. It was a collection of pictures of all the Miyagi karate *senseis*. Daniel knew that *sensei* (pronounced sen-say) was Japanese for *teacher* or *master*. There were about twenty pictures, but one was higher on the wall and larger than all the others.

24

"Who is he?" Daniel asked Mr. Miyagi.

"He is the Miyagi who brought karate to Okinawa from China many years ago."

"How did that happen?"

"Shimpo, for that was his name, was a fisherman. One day he fell asleep in his boat. When he woke up, the winds had carried him to China. Ten years later, he returned to Okinawa with a wife, two children, and the secret to the Miyagi family karate."

"What's the secret?" Daniel asked, surprised.

Mr. Miyagi walked over to the weapons cabinet and removed a drum. He handed it to Daniel. It was small, perhaps four inches across, and there was a handle sticking out lollipop style. At the sides, there were leather thongs with a wooden ball at the end of each thong. The thongs looked like arms, and the balls looked like hands.

Mr. Miyagi took the drum from Daniel and twirled it back and forth, making the wooden balls hit the drum.

Rat-tat-tat!

"I don't get it," Daniel said. "How can a drum be a karate secret?"

"Practice. You will understand in time," Mr. Miyagi told him. Daniel took the drum and tried to spin it as Mr. Miyagi had. The only sound he could make was *ka-thunk*! He decided that he would try to work with the drum later, by himself.

26

After all, Mr. Miyagi had always been right before about learning karate.

"Come, Daniel-san," Mr. Miyagi said. "Now time to go."

Daniel put the drum back into the cabinet and followed Mr. Miyagi out of the house.

They walked through the village, and Daniel had his first good look at Tome since they'd arrived. It was a small village, built on a hill by the sea. When Mr. Miyagi was a boy, the town had survived on its fishing industry. Now, Daniel could see that there were no fishing boats in the harbor. All that remained of the town's fishing industry was a tumbledown building with a broken sign that read: SATO CANNERY.

"What happened?" Daniel asked.

"Yukie told me that Sato's big commercial fishing boats took all the fish out of the waters here. Now all the fish are gone. Villagers have become farmers. They grow vegetables in their little gardens on land belonging to Sato and sell them to the market, owned by — "

"I know. Don't tell me. Sato owns the market, right?"

"Right. You learn fast, Daniel-san."

"So, Sato really owns this village, doesn't he?"

"*Hai*. The people of Tome are at his mercy."

And from what Daniel had seen, Sato didn't have much mercy.

8

Daniel and Mr. Miyagi continued walking through the town. They saw an old man teaching some children how to play instruments. The teacher and his students sat together on the steps of the wooden shrine in the center of town. Mr. Miyagi smiled when he saw them. He told Daniel that the man's name was Ichiro.

"The day I left Tome, forty-five years ago, Ichiro was in the same place, doing the same thing."

Daniel was interested to see how some things had changed very much in the village, and some things not at all. The fishermen had become farmers, but old Ichiro still taught their sons and daughters about music.

Down the street, Kumiko was in the school yard. She was teaching a group of young girls to dance. She waved at Daniel and Mr. Miyagi when they paused to watch her class.

At the end of the dance, they continued on down the street toward the harbor.

"Say, what's that?" Daniel asked. He was pointing to an underground fort on a hill. The gun ports overlooked the harbor.

"Must be a bunker left over from the war," Mr. Miyagi said. Then he asked a nearby villager about it in Japanese. "He tells me it's used as a storm shelter now," Mr. Miyagi translated for Daniel.

They continued their walk, but before they went far, they were stopped cold. Sato's big car pulled in front of them and screeched to a halt, blocking their way. Sato stepped out of the car and crossed his arms in front of his chest.

"You have seen your father," Sato said. "We will finish tonight. I will bring my nephew as witness."

Daniel was frightened by the challenge. Mr. Miyagi remained cool, though.

"Then the two of you will lose a night's sleep. I will not come," Mr. Miyagi told Sato.

Daniel could tell that Sato was furious. Sato had been waiting for the chance to fight Mr. Miyagi for forty-five years, and now Mr. Miyagi wouldn't fight. One look at Sato told Daniel that he was about to burst. Daniel thought about that powerful hand smashing through twelve boards. Now, it seemed that it might be about to smash through Mr. Miyagi!

However, before the explosion came, a voice interrupted them.

"Miyagi-san, Miyagi-san!" It was Yukie. She was running toward them all as fast as she could. She was nearly out of breath when she arrived. All she could say was, "Your father — he asks for you." She turned to Sato. "And you," she said.

Quickly, they all turned to go to Mr. Miyagi's father. When they entered the room and saw him, Daniel knew that the end was near. The old man could no longer speak, but he had something he wanted to say to Mr. Miyagi and Sato.

Each kneeled on either side of the bed. The dying man's weak hands reached for the hands of Sato and Mr. Miyagi. When each had taken one of his hands, he joined their hands together above him. It was his way of asking them to be friends once again — to forget the struggle between them.

Then the old man's hands fell to his side and his eyes fluttered and closed for the last time.

When Sato spoke, Daniel knew that the old man's dying request would not be honored. Sato said, "Out of respect for your father, I will leave you alone for a while. Then I will be back."

Daniel remembered the fury that was about to explode from Sato before Yukie had arrived. He wondered what Mr. Miyagi would do.

31

9

Mr. Miyagi spent a lot of time in the next few days by himself. At first, he was very sad. He was thinking about his father. He realized that he had always loved his father and that even though he had gone away, his father had always loved him, too. When he finally understood that, he knew it was more important for him to be happy at having seen his father again than it was for him to be sad about the old man's death.

Soon after that, he and Daniel started working again on Daniel's karate. Daniel got to use the Miyagi family *dojo*. The first day they were in the *dojo*, Mr. Miyagi put a picture of his father with the pictures of all the other Miyagi karate masters. He had certainly earned his place with the revered ancestors. Daniel and Mr. Miyagi stared at the group of pictures, admiring them. Daniel understood that Mr. Miyagi was very proud of his family.

Later that day, Daniel was taking a walk through the town of Tome. He liked the town and enjoyed watching the people work in it.

It was a harvest day in Tome and all the farmers were bringing their crops to Sato's market. Chozen and Taro, another of Sato's men, stood at the back of a big truck, parked by the road. They were weighing the vegetables and paying the farmers for them.

Then something caught Daniel's eye. It was the old man, Ichiro. He was struggling with a wheelbarrow filled with carrots. One of the wheels was stuck in a rut and he couldn't get it out. Daniel ran over to help him. Before he got there, the old man slipped and fell down. The wheelbarrow dumped the carrots all over the road.

Daniel helped Ichiro stand up, and asked him, "Are you okay?"

Ichiro looked at Daniel blankly. Daniel realized that Ichiro didn't speak any English. Daniel, however, had been studying a Japanese phrase book. This was the time to try it out.

"*Ikaga desu ka?*" Daniel asked. *How are you?*

The old man smiled. "*Genki desu.*" *I feel fine.*

Daniel was proud of himself, and the old man was pleased that Daniel had spoken to him in his own language. They had become friends with a few words and kind gestures. Daniel wished it were always so easy to become friends with people.

Daniel made sure that Ichiro was sitting comfortably. Then Daniel collected the carrots and put them back in the wheelbarrow. Daniel pushed the wheelbarrow over to the truck and waited in line to have Ichiro's carrots weighed.

When it was Daniel's turn, Chozen and Taro were talking to each other in Japanese and laughing cruelly while they looked at Daniel. Daniel knew they were making fun of him, but he also knew the best thing was to ignore it. Chozen made that impossible, though.

"I said your teacher should get a hearing aid," Chozen told him. Daniel pretended he couldn't hear. "Maybe you need one, too," Chozen continued.

"I only hear what's worth listening to," Daniel said, turning his attention to the scales.

It was an old-fashioned balance. The carrots were put on one side and weights were placed on the other. When they balanced, Taro figured out how much the weight was and paid the farmer for the vegetables.

Chozen handed the money to Ichiro, and Daniel lifted the carrots off the scale to put them in the truck. When he did that, though, he accidentally knocked the weights off the other side of the balance. He put the carrots into the truck and then leaned down to pick up the weights.

Right away, Daniel knew something was wrong. He'd been watching the procedure enough to know that the two small weights were supposed to equal the weight of the one big one. When he had the two in one hand and the big one in the other, though, they weren't the same at all.

He turned to Ichiro. *"Onaji?"* he asked, wanting to know if he was right that the two small weights should equal the big one. *Same?*

"Hai. Onaji mono desu," Ichiro replied. *Yes. They are the same.*

But they weren't. Daniel put the weights on the scale. The two weights were *much* heavier than the one, and that could mean only one thing: Chozen was cheating the farmers of Tome.

The farmers started yelling at Chozen, demanding that he reweigh their vegetables. Chozen agreed, reluctantly. Daniel watched him scowl as he paid each farmer the fair amount.

Daniel knew that he had done a good thing for the farmers of Tome. He wasn't so sure that he'd done a good thing for himself. He had certainly made an enemy of Chozen. He didn't want to think what that might mean.

10

After dinner that night, Daniel had a taste of the consequences for making Chozen look bad in front of Tome's farmers. But first, he had another lesson in friendship.

Daniel was sitting in the garden, studying Mr. Miyagi's drum. He twirled it and saw that it looked like a man, swinging his arms as he spun. Daniel set the drum down and tried to twirl like the drum. The faster he spun, the higher and harder his arms swung. It made him dizzy. It didn't make him feel any smarter about karate. He tried again.

This time when he stopped spinning, he was face-to-face with Kumiko.

"Hi," he said, startled.

"Hello. What are you doing?"

"Uh, practicing some moves, I think. Like for karate."

"Looks like the Bon Dance," she told him.

"What's that?" Daniel asked.

37

"That's an ancient traditional dance. We honor our dead with an annual festival. It comes up next month. Here," she offered. "I'll show you the dance."

Kumiko hummed a tune and began to dance gracefully. Daniel could see that the movement was a little like the drum movement he'd been trying. But he liked the way she did it much better.

"That looks great," he said.

"You try."

At first Daniel protested, but then he tried it and found that he liked it. He was a bit clumsy, but he got the idea and did what Kumiko did.

She smiled at him, encouraging him. "Good. Now to the right . . . and to the left . . . and turn. Very good, Daniel-san!"

Daniel followed Kumiko down the street, dancing all the way. He was having such fun that he didn't see Chozen until he stood in their way. Daniel twirled and found, with a start, that he was toe-to-toe with Chozen. Taro and Toshio stood next to him.

"You dance very nice," Chozen sneered. "Like a girl!"

Kumiko tugged at Daniel's hand. "Come, Daniel-san. Let's go."

Chozen laughed at Kumiko and Daniel.

"Listen, I'm not looking for any trouble," Daniel told Chozen.

"Well, maybe trouble is looking for you," Chozen said. He looked like he was going to attack Daniel with karate.

Daniel didn't move. "I'm not going to play your game," he told Chozen.

"It's not a game," Chozen said.

Daniel knew Chozen was serious, but he stood his ground. Chozen shoved him.

"Cut it out!" Daniel warned.

Chozen shoved Daniel again and that made Daniel forget that he didn't want to fight Chozen. He wanted to attack. He charged at Chozen, trying to punch. But Chozen was ready for him. He sidestepped, evading the punch. Then he kicked Daniel in the stomach. Daniel doubled over in pain.

"Next time you insult my honor, you are dead," Chozen told him. Then he and his henchmen turned and walked down the street.

"Are you okay?" Kumiko asked, helping Daniel to stand.

"Yeah. But I don't know how he figures it."

"Figures what?"

"He cheats the farmers of Tome and then accuses me of insulting his honor."

"He has no idea what honor is," Kumiko said.

"I kind of got that feeling," Daniel said.

It was a bad feeling, too.

11

The next morning, Daniel was up early, working out in the *dojo*. He practiced the drum movement, trying to make it more like karate than dancing. After a while, he realized that if he were trying to punch while he twirled, he'd be able to hit someone very hard. The spinning made his arms swing with a lot of force.

"Good morning, Daniel-san." It was Mr. Miyagi. "What are you doing?"

"Experimenting. Want to see something?" he asked. Mr. Miyagi nodded.

Daniel stood still, arms at his sides. Then, as he had practiced, he stepped forward and to the left with his left foot. He lifted his right foot from the ground and spun on his left toe. His arms swung out, more powerfully than before.

"How'd you like that?"

"Very good, Daniel-san. I knew you could unravel the secret of the drum. Now try this." Mr.

41

Miyagi demonstrated. He shifted his weight to both feet, using his hips. Daniel tried it. The movement was even more powerful.

Then it was time for Daniel to stop.

"Kumiko's taking me around the island for a tour today, if it's okay with you," he told Mr. Miyagi.

"That's okay with me," he said. "We'll meet you later in the city. I have to change the deed on this house. I'm giving it to Yukie."

"Great. We'll see you about four o'clock." They agreed on a place and Daniel left to get ready to meet Kumiko.

The first stop on Daniel's tour with Kumiko was an ancient castle that stood on a cliff at the edge of the sea.

"These are the ruins of the castle of King Shohashi. The name of the place is the Castle of Courtesy and Good Manners."

"Why is it called that?" Daniel asked.

Kumiko pointed out over the water. "See there?" she asked. Then she pointed the other way. "And there? On one side is China. The other side is Japan. Okinawa lives between two giants. The only way we survive is by having courtesy and good manners."

Daniel laughed because it was funny, but his recent brush with Chozen had taught him that

42

sometimes even having courtesy and good manners wouldn't save you from a fight.

"And over here." She pointed to the inside of the castle. "Every summer for eight hundred years, the Bon Dance and Festival was held here. But no more." She looked sad.

"Why?" Daniel asked.

"Sato," she explained. "He owns the castle. He sells it. Piece by piece. Now you see, it is only a ruin."

"Can't somebody stop him?" Daniel thought it was terribly unfair.

"Nobody can stop him — just as nobody could stop him from taking all the fish from the water. He uses everything he owns and then discards it when he has destroyed it."

Daniel thought about that and he knew it was true. He was very afraid of what that might mean to the town of Tome. He was even more worried about what it would mean to his friend, Mr. Miyagi.

12

Daniel thought Naha City was fascinating. It was the oddest mix of ancient Okinawa and modern America that he could have imagined. The traffic was a confusion of U.S. military jeeps and trucks with Okinawan cars, bicycles, and pedicabs.

Kumiko guided Daniel through the mass of people and cars. He stared at the Okinawan grocery store, which had unfamiliar foods in the window. Right next door, however, was an American fried-chicken fast-food restaurant. Next to that was a video store.

As they walked along the sidewalk, a young man handed Kumiko a piece of paper.

"Hey!" Kumiko said, reading it. "There's a rock 'n' roll dance tomorrow night. Would you like to go?"

"Sure. That'll be fun."

Just at that moment, something caught his eye.

It was a large storefront building. The sign on the building said it was: WORLD HEADQUARTERS — MASTER SATO — OKINAWAN KARATE. Inside, Daniel could see a class going on. He saw Chozen teaching Americans by fighting with them, two at a time. He was also beating them, two at a time. Chozen was very good at karate.

"Come on now, Daniel-san. It's almost time to meet Miyagi-san."

Daniel walked away from the karate school, following Kumiko along the crowded sidewalk. But then something else caught his attention.

Daniel and Kumiko heard loud laughter from inside an arcade. Daniel went into the dark building. Kumiko followed him. When they got to the source of the noise, Daniel saw a crowd of people, mostly men. It was a kind of informal tournament. One by one, the men were trying to break a rack of three thick cakes of ice with a single karate chop.

As each man tried it, the men in the crowd were betting whether he would be able to do it. None of them could do it, but still they kept on trying, and kept on hurting their hands on the ice cakes.

Daniel and Kumiko saw one really strong-looking man. He rubbed his bulging muscles to loosen them for action. Daniel could see that he was strong, but it didn't seem that the man was using his brain. Daniel knew that the secret to karate was

in the head, not the muscles. The man prepared to chop at the ice.

"He's not going to do it," Daniel whispered to Kumiko. The man heard Daniel and was annoyed. He gave Daniel a very dirty look. Then he flexed his muscles again, raised his arm, and shot it through the air at the ice. When his hand hit the ice, the ice didn't break.

"Yeow!" the man yelled in pain, holding his bruised hand gently. "You think you could do better, big mouth?" he asked Daniel.

Daniel shrugged and said, "I couldn't do worse." The minute he spoke, he was sorry, because when he started to leave, there was Chozen to stop him. Daniel didn't know how Chozen had gotten there, but he knew his arrival was bad news.

"Let's see how you chop the ice cakes, Mr. U.S. Karate Champ," Chozen said.

"Maybe some other time," Daniel said, trying to get out.

"There is no other time," Chozen said.

Daniel knew he meant it.

13

Daniel wondered how he had gotten himself into such trouble this time. Even more, he wondered how he was going to get *out* of it. Sure, he knew a lot about karate. He'd studied hard with Mr. Miyagi. But he didn't know anything about chopping blocks of ice!

Just when he thought things couldn't get worse, Chozen started taking bets. He was betting that Daniel couldn't even chop through *one* block of ice. Daniel was afraid he was right. But his own honor was at stake. He stared glumly at the fresh rack of ice on the table before him.

Then, he heard a familiar voice in the crowd. It was Mr. Miyagi! He'd know what to do. He'd know how to get Daniel out of this mess. Daniel was sure that Mr. Miyagi would save him — until he heard Mr. Miyagi speak to Chozen.

"I'll bet four hundred dollars!" Mr. Miyagi said. Daniel couldn't believe it. What could Mr. Miyagi be thinking?

The crowd started chanting to encourage Daniel.

"One second," he said, asking for a delay. He turned to Mr. Miyagi and whispered, "What do I do now?"

Once again, Mr. Miyagi surprised Daniel. "Focus," he told Daniel. "That's all our money I just bet on you."

"Great," Daniel said. "And what are *you* going to do?"

"Pray." Mr. Miyagi put both his hands in front of him in the prayer position. There was something very familiar about it. Then Daniel understood. He knew what he had to do. He nodded at Mr. Miyagi, smiling.

He stood in front of the blocks of ice. He put his hands in the prayer position, too. He had to return to the basic of life. He remembered how Mr. Miyagi had taught him to breathe. He breathed in and then out, raising his hands. He breathed in again, returning his hands to the prayer position. Then he breathed out, reaching in front of himself. Breathing in, he returned his hands. He performed the exercise again and a final time. By then he had focused all his attention on the ice.

He really didn't see the people around him. He really didn't hear the noise of the crowd. He could no longer smell the smoky air or feel the heat in the room. The only thing he could see was the ice.

The only other thing he was sure of in the whole world was that his hand could break through it.

He raised his right hand in the air and breathed in. Breathing out, he slashed downward at the ice. Daniel heard the ice cracking before he saw it, and then he saw it before he felt it. He had cut all three cakes of ice in half! Nobody else had been able to do even *one*.

The crowd roared in approval. Daniel looked at Chozen. Chozen was furious. He didn't like Daniel's success. Even more, he didn't like the fact that he had lost so much money betting. Chozen made a face as he paid the winners. When he got to Mr. Miyagi, he tried to weasel out of the bet.

"We do not honor bets with cowards!" Chozen told Mr. Miyagi. But Sato was there, too. He was angry that Chozen would try to cheat anyone — even his old enemy.

"Do not embarrass me," he told Chozen. "Pay Miyagi-san." Reluctantly, Chozen gave the money to Mr. Miyagi.

Daniel knew it was time to go. He and Kumiko left quickly with Mr. Miyagi.

There had been enough trouble for one day. Daniel actually thought there had been enough trouble for a lifetime, but he had the feeling there was more to come.

He was right.

14

The next day was the day of the rock 'n' roll dance that Daniel and Kumiko were going to attend. Daniel was glad to be doing something with Kumiko. He liked her very much.

"*Komban wa!*" she said, entering the garden where Daniel and Mr. Miyagi were talking. *Good evening.*

"*Komban wa,*" Daniel said in return, bowing to her.

She smiled at the way he was learning Japanese manners. "Here, this is for you," she said, handing him a bag.

"What is it?"

"Dance clothes for the rock 'n' roll dance. Try them on."

"Dance clothes?" Daniel didn't understand.

"*Hai,*" she said, but before she could explain, there was an interruption.

"Miyagi! Miyagi!" With a sinking feeling, Daniel

recognized Chozen's voice. They turned to see Chozen, Taro, and Toshio enter the garden. Each of them held hoes in their hands. Their yelling had attracted many of Mr. Miyagi's neighbors who came to see what was going to happen.

Chozen spoke to Mr. Miyagi. "My uncle says his obligation to your father's memory is fulfilled. He waits at his *dojo*. I have been sent to get you."

"Tell him I am a farmer, not a fighter," Mr. Miyagi told Chozen.

Chozen nodded at Taro and Toshio. All three of them began chopping up the plants in Mr. Miyagi's garden. It was just a small vegetable patch. Within a very few seconds, it was completely destroyed.

"Now farming is finished," Chozen announced.

Mr. Miyagi didn't answer him. Instead, he got down on his hands and knees and began to clear the patch.

"What are you doing?" Chozen demanded.

"Replanting," Mr. Miyagi told him.

Chozen was angry, but he knew he couldn't convince Mr. Miyagi. Chozen, Taro, and Toshio turned and marched out of the vegetable patch.

Mr. Miyagi's neighbors helped him to clear the patch. Within a few minutes, it was ready for replanting. When the work was done, Mr. Miyagi told Daniel and Kumiko it was time for them to get ready for the dance.

Daniel had almost forgotten about the dance. He had forgotten about the bagful of clothes Kumiko had brought him. He and Kumiko went into separate rooms in the house to get ready. Daniel had quite a surprise when he opened the bag. It was full of old fifties' style clothes: blue jeans, white T-shirt, Hawaiian shirt, cowboy belt, and black high-top basketball sneakers. He really looked funny when he got dressed. But he looked even funnier by the time Kumiko had combed his hair! She put a lot of goo on it and combed it back up so that he *really* looked like he came from the fifties.

At the same time, Kumiko had put on her own fifties' outfit. She wore pedal pushers and a halter top. Her shoes were high heels with fur trim. Her hair was in a ponytail. She looked very *un*-Japanese. He laughed when he saw her.

"Don't you think we're going to kind of stand out in the crowd?" he asked.

"Lucky if we get noticed at all," she told him.

She was right about that!

15

Daniel was amazed by the collection of clothes at the dance. It was almost as funny as a Halloween dance, except that at one time — in the fifties — people had actually dressed like that! Some of the girls wore skirts with poodles on them, and wide elastic belts. One girl even had brown and white saddle shoes. Some of the boys were dressed like Daniel. Others looked more "preppy." None of them looked Japanese.

Kumiko was a very good dancer. She was good at the Bon Dance, but she was also good at the lindy and the fox trot. She taught Daniel how to do the dances. He was really having a good time. He always had a good time with Kumiko. She was a very special friend to him.

Just when Daniel was beginning to think he could forget about all the bad things that had been happening lately, Chozen showed up at the dance. Daniel was so angry to see him that he forgot to

wonder how he'd known Daniel and Kumiko would be at the dance. Chozen, Taro, and Toshio confronted Daniel on the dance floor.

"What do you want from me now?" Daniel asked.

"I want my money back," Chozen said, holding out his hand.

"I won it. Fair and square."

But being right was never enough for Chozen. When the music got loud and the other people on the dance floor weren't looking, Chozen punched Daniel in the stomach. Daniel doubled over in pain. Taro and Toshio grabbed him and pulled the money out of his pocket.

"That's all my money!" Daniel protested.

Chozen took two bills off the stack and dropped them on the floor for Daniel. When Taro and Toshio released Daniel, he kneeled down to pick up the money. But as soon as he had the money in his hand, he sprang upward in an attack at Chozen. Chozen was completely unprepared for Daniel's attack. He was so surprised that he dropped Daniel's money as he fell onto the dance floor.

Quickly, Daniel reached for the money with one hand and for Kumiko with the other. Before Chozen could even stand up, Daniel and Kumiko had left the dance and were safely out of sight.

Once again, Daniel knew that he had won a battle against Chozen. But he also knew that the war was not over.

16

Daniel woke up with a start. At first, he couldn't remember where he was. Then it came to him. Mr. Miyagi had gone fishing the night before, so Daniel was alone in the house. He'd slept in the *dojo*. Before he went to sleep, though, he'd taken a spear from the weapons cabinet. All night, it was at his side — just in case.

Crash! Bang! Thud!

What could the noise be? Daniel jumped up from the mat and went to the garden. There stood Sato.

"Where is Miyagi?"

"I don't know," Daniel told him truthfully.

At that moment Chozen appeared, along with Taro and Toshio. They carried hammers and axes. Daniel realized that the noises he'd heard were those three, damaging the house! Was there no end to this? Daniel wondered.

"Miyagi is not here, Uncle," Chozen reported.

Sato scowled. "Destroy the garden," he ordered

Chozen. Then he turned and left, leaving Chozen and his cohorts to do his dirty work.

The day before, Chozen had ruined the vegetable patch. Now he and his friends were ruining the beautiful garden. It was planted with bonsai trees that were hundreds of years old. Though it had taken hundreds of years to grow the miniature trees, it was taking Chozen only a few seconds to destroy them. Daniel couldn't stand it anymore.

He still held the spear in his hand. He began to attack Taro, but Chozen was in his way. Chozen tripped Daniel. Daniel scrambled to his feet. He pointed the spear at his attackers.

"What are you going to do with that, little coward?" said Chozen.

"Come and find out," Daniel challenged.

"I will," Chozen told him.

Chozen lunged at Daniel. Daniel tried to stop him with the spear, but Chozen ducked under it. He came up behind Daniel and before Daniel knew what was happening, Chozen had grabbed the spear and was choking Daniel with it!

Daniel knew he was in real trouble now. He knew that he didn't have a chance alone against these three. Daniel couldn't breathe at all. He felt very dizzy and weak. He was barely aware of what was happening around him. Suddenly, though, Chozen let go. Daniel didn't know why. Gratefully, he slid to his knees and tried to see what was going on.

He realized that someone else had come into the garden. Someone else was attacking. He was attacking Chozen, Taro, and Toshio all at the same time. He was beating them, too!

Punch! Kick! Chop! Kiaiiii! Thud! Taro landed on the ground. Two more quick kicks, and Toshio joined him in the dirt. Daniel tried harder to focus his eyes. He wanted to know who had come to help him. As his rescuer attacked Chozen, Daniel finally realized who it was. It was Mr. Miyagi!

Daniel could see that Chozen had the spear. Chozen tried to attack Mr. Miyagi with it. When he lunged, Mr. Miyagi grabbed the end of the spear and lifted it high in the air, picking Chozen up with it! Chozen dangled above the garden. He was terrified. Mr. Miyagi dropped the spear, making Chozen land very hard. He was completely beaten by Mr. Miyagi. As soon as Chozen could stand up, he and his friends ran from Mr. Miyagi's garden in defeat. Just at that moment, Kumiko and Yukie arrived in the garden.

"Are you all right, Daniel-san?" Mr. Miyagi asked. Daniel could only nod. His throat hurt a lot, but he knew he was okay.

"Stay here," Mr. Miyagi told him, walking toward the gate.

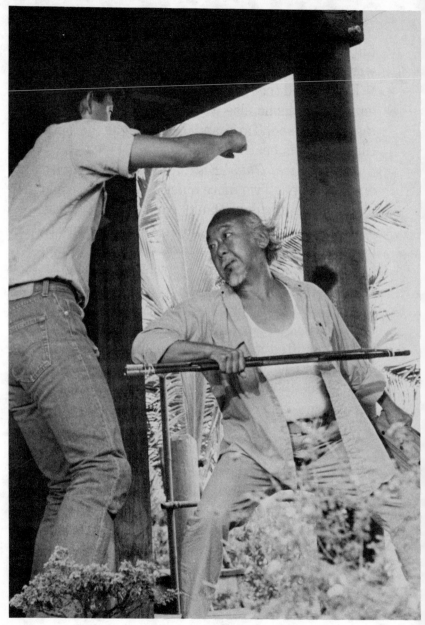

62

"Where are you going?" Daniel whispered.

"I am going to put an end to this," he said.

Daniel scrambled to his feet. He thought Mr. Miyagi meant to go have it out with Sato. He couldn't let him go alone! He ran after Mr. Miyagi, but Mr. Miyagi had already driven his car out of the driveway.

Daniel knew what he had to do. "Kumiko," he said. "You must take me where Mr. Miyagi has gone."

At first, she didn't want to, but she realized that Daniel felt he had to be with Mr. Miyagi. She was also afraid he would get lost if he tried to drive after Mr. Miyagi by himself. Together they drove after Mr. Miyagi's speeding car.

Daniel wondered how this would all end.

17

When they finally caught up with Mr. Miyagi, he was just stepping out of a shop in Naha City. But it wasn't Sato's *dojo*. It was a travel agency. Then Daniel realized that Mr. Miyagi's solution to his problem with Sato was to leave Okinawa again.

Daniel couldn't believe it. Were Sato and Chozen right? Maybe Mr. Miyagi *was* a coward. Could it be true? Daniel had to know. He jumped out of Kumiko's car and ran over to Mr. Miyagi.

"You're leaving?" he asked.

"*We're* leaving," Mr. Miyagi corrected him.

"I don't understand, Mr. Miyagi," Daniel said. "When I had all that trouble before with those bullies in California, you told me to stand up to them."

"I told you to face reality," Mr. Miyagi said.

"What about *you* facing it?"

"I am."

"No, you're not. You're running away."

"Do you think I am afraid, Daniel-san?"

That was the question. It was the question Daniel had asked himself earlier. It was the question he was still asking himself.

Daniel turned and walked away from Mr. Miyagi and Kumiko. He needed to be by himself to think. Alone, he walked down the street.

Daniel walked for a long time. He didn't notice anything or anyone around him. All he saw was the sidewalk in front of him and all he thought about was Mr. Miyagi. Was he a coward? Was he running away from Sato? What good would it do anyone if Mr. Miyagi did fight Sato? What good would it do Mr. Miyagi if he left Okinawa?

Daniel thought about these things very hard. He knew there were no easy answers. They were hard questions.

After a long time, he stopped walking and stood by a store. He was staring into the window, but at first, he didn't really know what he was seeing. Soon, though, he began to understand.

The store was an Army-Navy surplus store. It sold everything from disarmed rifles and machine guns to used medals. These were the tools and symbols of bravery, weren't they? Daniel asked himself. He stepped into the store.

Inside, two American GI's were playing with a binful of weapons. The weapons were real, all right, but they'd been fixed so they couldn't shoot.

"Pow! Pow! I'm killing the enemy!" one of the men said, shooting at imaginary bad guys.

"Pop! Ka*boom*!" said the other, launching an imaginary grenade at the same bad guys.

Daniel watched as these grown men played with the real weapons. It made him think of little kids playing cops and robbers or GI Joe. But these weren't little kids, these were men. Just like Sato and Chozen were men.

Then Daniel understood. Sato and Chozen were grown-up, but they were still playing like kids. The only difference was that their weapons were real. Their karate could kill! If Mr. Miyagi fought with Sato, he'd be just another grown man playing like a kid but with a real weapon.

That was the answer, then: It was time to go home. Mr. Miyagi was right. No good would be done by staying in Okinawa any longer — only harm.

Daniel turned to leave the store. He saw that Mr. Miyagi was standing outside waiting for him. Daniel smiled at him. Mr. Miyagi smiled back.

Daniel went outside to be with his friend. He was ready to go home.

18

Daniel and Mr. Miyagi had just finished packing their suitcases when they heard the noise. It was the grinding, screeching sound of big trucks and bulldozers. They ran outside of the house to see what was happening. It seemed like the whole village had come to watch, too, for the street was full of people.

What they saw was a line of big yellow construction trucks carrying men and tools to destroy the village! One of the bulldozers was beginning to ruin Mr. Miyagi's neighbor's garden. Each truck had written on its side: SATO CONSTRUCTION.

Sato was with the crew.

Mr. Miyagi ran up to him. "What are you doing?" he yelled.

"I am selling the land," Sato told him.

"Why?"

"Why do you think?"

Daniel realized how deep Sato's hatred was. He

was willing to destroy the entire village to get back at Mr. Miyagi.

"You will destroy the village!"

"No, Miyagi-san, *you* will."

Daniel knew then that Sato would get what he wanted. Mr. Miyagi could not let him ruin the village.

"You win. I will fight," Mr. Miyagi told him. "But on one condition."

"What?"

"Regardless of who wins, the deed to all this land passes from you to the village."

Sato wanted to fight Mr. Miyagi so much that he agreed. "It will be done. I will see you here. At midnight." He turned to leave, but stopped to warn Mr. Miyagi. "No tricks. Or this is gone." He pointed to all the land in the village. "Their school. Their homes. All of it." He gave an order to his men. "Leave the equipment." Then he walked down the street, turning his back on Mr. Miyagi and the rest of the villagers.

Mr. Miyagi and Daniel returned to the house.

"I don't suppose you'd consider leaving now, would you?" Daniel asked.

"Daniel-san, don't worry," Mr. Miyagi said, comforting him.

"How can I not worry? Sato is like a kid playing at war games. The only difference is that his weap-

ons are real. I mean, I know what happens if you lose."

"But I have already won, Daniel-san. Whatever happens to me, the village is saved forever. Sato can never threaten these people's lives again. Their land is theirs now. Not his. I must prepare now."

Mr. Miyagi went upstairs to change his clothes. Daniel knew that Mr. Miyagi would spend the rest of the day and the evening until midnight by himself, meditating in the *dojo*.

Daniel couldn't be so calm, and he knew that he couldn't help Mr. Miyagi. He needed a friend. He wanted to see Kumiko, to talk with her.

"Where is Kumiko?" he asked Yukie.

"She is waiting for you, Daniel-san. At the cannery."

Daniel wondered why Kumiko would be at the cannery — waiting for him. Whatever the reason, it sounded better than staying at Mr. Miyagi's. He left the house and walked down the street to meet Kumiko.

19

Daniel walked past the village shrine on his way to the cannery. Inside the shrine, he saw Sato, meditating the same way Mr. Miyagi was meditating in his *dojo*. Daniel thought it was sad that these two men had so much in common but still had to fight each other. He shook his head in sorrow and continued to the cannery.

A brisk wind blew at his face. The leaves fluttered on the trees. Inside the cannery, Daniel could hear the musical tinkle of a wind chime. He followed the sound.

"Kumiko?" he called.

He found her before she could answer — and what a surprise she had for him! There, in the abandoned cannery, she had set up a table to serve tea, complete with china, silk decorations, and flowers. She was dressed in an old-fashioned Japanese kimono. When she saw Daniel, she asked him to sit at the table. Then she served him.

Daniel had heard about tea ceremonies, but he never thought he'd be part of one. He watched, fascinated, as Kumiko prepared everything for him perfectly. The ceremony was so beautiful that Daniel barely even noticed how good the tea tasted. This was a real treat for him.

But then Daniel and Kumiko heard the wind chime rattle again. This time it wasn't a gentle tinkle. It was an urgent clang. Kumiko looked out the window. When she saw how the wind was tugging at the trees, a look of fear came over her face.

"Quickly," she said to Daniel, collecting all the tea things and putting them into her carrying box. "We have no time, Daniel."

Daniel was confused and worried. What was going on? he wondered as they hurried out of the cannery. He didn't have to wonder for long. In a second it was pouring rain. The wind pushed the rain into their faces, making it very hard to see and to walk up the hill.

Daniel carried the box and held Kumiko's hand to help her walk up the hill.

"Does it get worse?" he asked her.

"Much worse," she said. "It's a typhoon."

Then Daniel was afraid.

20

"Come, Daniel-san," Kumiko said. "We will go to the shelter." Daniel remembered the storm shelter he'd seen his first day in Tome. It was the old fortified bunker, left from World War II. Now Daniel understood why the town needed a storm shelter. In the sun on that first day, it had seemed a joke. This day, Daniel knew it was no joke. Daniel hoped they could get to it safely.

There was a bell tower near the shelter. A young boy was in the tower. He was ringing the bell as loudly and as furiously as he could. He wanted to warn all the people of Tome about the storm. He wanted to guide them to the storm shelter. *Ding-dong! Ding-dong! Ding-dong!*

Kumiko and Daniel met up with Yukie and Mr. Miyagi by the door to the shelter. They were relieved to see each other and to know they were all safe. Daniel and Mr. Miyagi helped the villagers into the shelter.

Suddenly there was a whip of wind, harder than before. It struck at the shrine where Sato and Chozen were. The wind pulled the shrine from its foundation. The whole thing collapsed. Chozen came running out of the debris and fled to the shelter.

Mr. Miyagi stopped him. "Where is your uncle?" he asked.

"Dead," Chozen said, and escaped inside.

Battling the fierce wind and driving rain, Mr. Miyagi ran toward the ruins of the shrine. Daniel followed him. As they got to it, the wind ripped away the collapsed roof. They could see Sato. He was stuck under a big piece of wood. He was alive.

Quickly, Daniel and Mr. Miyagi went to rescue him. Sato couldn't believe they would help him, though. He was sure Mr. Miyagi would take the opportunity to kill him. When Daniel saw the fear in Sato's face, he knew that Sato didn't know Mr. Miyagi very well.

The only way Mr. Miyagi could rescue Sato was to chop the wood that held him. Daniel remembered the picture of Sato in the airport, chopping the twelve pieces of wood. He wondered if Mr. Miyagi could do it. This one log was much thicker than all twelve pieces Sato had chopped.

Sato closed his eyes, expecting the death blow. Mr. Miyagi raised his hand and then slashed it through the air.

"*Kiiaiiiii!*" he cried. His hand chopped the wood

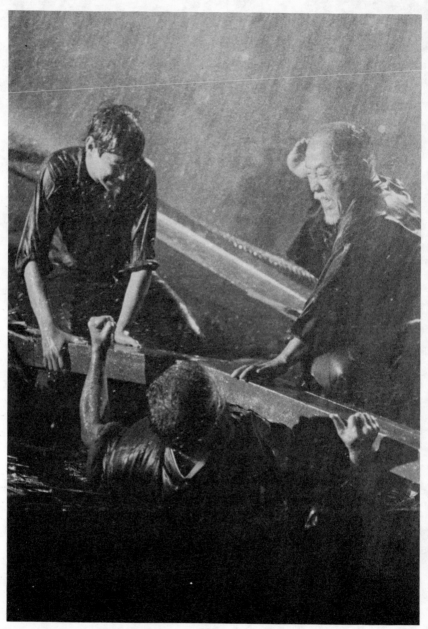

with a fierce blow, and the whole beam broke in two pieces. As soon as they could remove the pieces of broken beam, Daniel and Mr. Miyagi helped Sato stand and walk to the storm shelter. Sato could not believe his good fortune. When the three of them were safely inside, Sato bowed deeply to Mr. Miyagi and Daniel. The people of the village were surprised. So was Daniel. He knew that Sato's bow of respect meant that Sato was no longer angry at Mr. Miyagi. Their battle was done. Mr. Miyagi had won!

Then Chozen came over to his uncle. He was very embarrassed that he had left him for dead at the shrine.

"Uncle. I thought you were dead — " he started to explain.

But Sato interrupted him. "You left me for dead? Then, to you, that's what I am! You may no longer speak to me or see me. As far as you're concerned, I no longer exist!"

With that, he turned his back on Chozen. Chozen was so surprised and hurt that he could not bear to be in the shelter. He ran out into the storm by himself. Within seconds he had disappeared into the night.

21

When morning came, the storm was all over. All over, that is, except for the big repair job that would have to be done on the village. The villagers left the shelter and returned to their homes to begin their tasks.

Mr. Miyagi and Daniel were working on Mr. Miyagi's house when they once again heard the rumble of trucks. This time it was different, though.

The trucks still said SATO CONSTRUCTION, and Sato was still with them, but this time he had a smile on his face.

"*Ohayo*," he said to Mr. Miyagi. "*Koko desu.*" *Hello. Here it is*, he said, handing Mr. Miyagi a scroll. "It is the deed to the land. I beg your forgiveness, old friend." He bowed deeply to Mr. Miyagi.

"There is nothing to forgive," Mr. Miyagi told him, accepting the scroll happily. The villagers cheered for the two friends. They cheered because now they owned their own land. They cheered because the storm was over and they were alive. It was a happy day in Tome.

Daniel knew there was one more thing the villagers wanted from Sato. He was scared to ask, but he knew he had to try.

"Uh, Mr. Sato," he began.

Sato turned to him.

"You know, the Bon Dance and Festival is soon and it will be hard to have it in the village — "

"What are you asking of me?"

Daniel swallowed.

"The castle. Where the dance really belongs, anyway. Can we have it there?"

Sato turned to Mr. Miyagi. "Your student becomes my teacher," he said. Then he spoke to Daniel and all of the villagers. "The Bon Dance will be held in the castle every year — " the villagers cheered again " — under one condition." There was silence. They waited for the bad news. "The condition is that Daniel-san dances!"

"You got it!" Daniel said, and reached out his hand to Sato. They sealed the deal with a shake.

22

The night of the Bon Dance was a night of great celebration for the people of Tome. The storm was over. Their homes were repaired. Their land belonged to them. Sato was their friend. They were grateful for all the good things Daniel and Mr. Miyagi had done.

The villagers gathered in the castle. It was old and a bit run-down, but they were happy to be there. They sat in a circle around the stage to watch the dancing. The floor between the audience and the stage had collapsed over the years. Until Sato was able to repair it, the only way to reach the stage was by a makeshift bridge of two boards spanning over a deep hole.

All the dancers, including Daniel, walked carefully over the bridge. When they reached the stage, the music began and they started to dance. Slowly, carefully, Daniel danced. He did all the steps just as Kumiko had taught him. It was a nice dance, not too hard. The villagers in the audience had little hand drums, like the one in Mr. Miyagi's *dojo*, which they twirled softly in time to the music.

In a very few minutes, Daniel's dance was over. The villagers clapped happily and banged their drums while Daniel and the dancers walked back over the little bridge. When they were all sitting down, the lights dimmed for a moment. As the lights brightened again, Kumiko appeared alone on the stage. It was the highlight of the evening. Kumiko was going to dance alone.

The music began. Kumiko started her dance. Daniel could not believe what a wonderful dancer she was. She moved so smoothly, so gracefully, it almost seemed as if she were moved by the gentle breezes of the night. Everyone in the audience was fascinated watching her.

In fact, they were so fascinated watching her that they didn't see the shadowy figure lurking in the darkness by the castle wall. They didn't see the shadowy figure slink down the aisle toward the stage. They didn't see the figure approach the little bridge and skulk across it.

Suddenly, the figure jumped at Kumiko and attacked her. He held her from behind with a knife at her throat! When he looked up at the audience, they could see it was Chozen.

"Where is Daniel?" he demanded.

"Stop this!" Sato called to Chozen.

But Chozen replied, "I cannot hear you, Uncle. You are dead to me, remember?"

Daniel knew that he had to face Chozen. It was the only way to save Kumiko.

"I'm here," he said, standing up.

"Cross the bridge," Chozen told him.

Daniel stepped over to the bridge and crossed it. Now he, Chozen, and Kumiko were alone on the stage.

"All right, I crossed the bridge. Now let her go."

Still holding Kumiko, Chozen stepped over toward the little bridge. With his foot, he kicked at the boards, shoving them over the edge of the stage. Daniel heard the boards clatter noisily to the bottom of the deep hole between the stage and the audience.

Then Chozen let Kumiko go. He pushed her aside, throwing her to the ground. He threw the knife into the deep hole where the boards had gone.

"What do you want?" Daniel asked him.

"Revenge," Chozen said.

23

Daniel looked at Chozen's icy stare. He wondered if he could possibly talk his way out of this. He didn't want to fight Chozen if he could avoid it. Mr. Miyagi had taught him that fighting was always the last — and worst — answer to a problem.

"Everything's been settled," he told Chozen.

"Everything but me. I hold *you* responsible for what happened to me." He started walking toward Daniel. "I have been embarrassed, humiliated, and dishonored. All because of you."

"Look," Daniel said. "For whatever happened, I apologize."

"Apology will not give me back my honor." Chozen continued to walk toward Daniel. Daniel stepped backward carefully.

"I'm not fighting," he said to Chozen.

"You're not running away this time, either," Chozen told him. Daniel knew that was true. He had nowhere to run. In fact, he was at the edge of the stage, the edge of the deep hole, the edge of big trouble.

Daniel knew he had no choice. He charged at Chozen, kicking and chopping at him with a punch. Chozen defended himself easily and was unhurt by Daniel's attack.

Mr. Miyagi cried out to Daniel from the audience. "Daniel-san, this is not a tournament. This is for *real*."

"Yes, for *very* real," Chozen threatened. Then Daniel was frightened.

Daniel attacked again, this time kicking with all his might. Chozen caught Daniel's foot before it hit, and pushed him away — to the edge of the stage. Daniel scrambled to keep from falling off, but Chozen kept pushing. Just when Daniel thought he couldn't hold out any longer, Kumiko came and pulled Chozen away. It didn't stop Chozen, but it gave Daniel a chance to move away from the edge.

Chozen threw Kumiko to the ground. Her head hit a stone and Daniel could see she was hurt. He didn't mind if Chozen hurt him, but he couldn't stand to see him hurt Kumiko. Daniel attacked again. He knew he had to win.

Daniel lunged, punching, and Chozen blocked the punches with his hands. He grabbed Daniel and threw him against a stone pillar on the stage. Then he tried a punch, but Daniel moved to the

side just in time. Chozen's fist hit the stone instead. He made a terrible face. Daniel knew it hurt.

Daniel stepped around Chozen, to attack, but Chozen spun around and punched Daniel, pushing him against the pillar again. Daniel slid down to the ground. Chozen jumped into the air with a flying kick at Daniel, but Daniel rolled to the side. Before Chozen could land, Daniel grabbed Chozen's leg in midair and threw him to the ground.

Daniel again lunged at Chozen, punching, but Chozen had scrambled to his feet. He grabbed Daniel's arm and swung him around, putting his whole arm around Daniel's neck. He held Daniel's arms behind him. Daniel was helpless. Chozen held him in a death grip!

24

Daniel was almost out of breath. He didn't know what to do. Chozen held him tightly and Daniel couldn't break the grip.

"Step back, Daniel-san!" Mr. Miyagi called from the audience. "Step back. Use hips."

Yes, that was it! Daniel stepped back into Chozen's stance and then leaned forward. The motion picked Chozen up off his feet. He flew straight over Daniel's head and landed on the ground with a thump. The death grip was broken!

Now Daniel punched and kicked at Chozen as he had never done before. All his karate training was coming into use. He had to use it — to save his life, and Kumiko's. But Chozen was good. Everything Daniel tried, Chozen blocked. And everything Chozen tried, Daniel blocked. At first, it seemed like neither one could possibly win.

But then, Mr. Miyagi gave Daniel just the help he needed.

Mr. Miyagi started twirling his drum. *Rat-tat-tat!* it went. The other people in the audience did the same. Daniel realized it was a message for him. Then he remembered. The drum was the secret of the Miyagi family karate. It was time to use the secret.

For a final time, Chozen lunged to attack Daniel. But Daniel was ready. He stood firmly in place and he began to swing from his waist, just like the drum. His arms were lifted with the swinging motion. Just as Chozen reached Daniel, Daniel's swinging right arm blocked the attack. Daniel's left hand followed with a punch. By the time Chozen attacked again, Daniel was twirling back. This time he blocked with his left hand and punched with the right. Again and again Daniel twirled back and forth, blocking and attacking. There was no way Chozen could overcome him. Within seconds, Chozen had fallen to the ground, beaten.

Daniel stepped over to him and grabbed Chozen's collar with his left hand. He brought his right hand back, threatening to give Chozen a final punch.

"Live or die," Daniel said to Chozen. "Your choice."

"Die."

But Daniel knew better. He had learned from Mr. Miyagi what honor really meant — and it didn't mean killing. If Sato could learn from Mr. Miyagi's teaching, Chozen could learn from Daniel. Daniel wouldn't give him the choice of death. That would only show that Daniel had no honor.

"Wrong," he told Chozen. "You must live. You must learn what honor *really* is. You must learn what courage is. Death is not the answer."

With that, Daniel stood up. He ran over to where Kumiko lay. He helped her stand up. She was hurt, but he knew she would be okay.

The villagers cheered for Daniel. Sato cheered for him. Kumiko cheered for him. But the one who cheered the loudest was Mr. Miyagi. He knew that by the example of his own courage and honor, he had taught Daniel well.

Then it seemed to Daniel that everything was going right. He knew that he had been able to help Mr. Miyagi and the villagers of Tome, and that he had been able to save Kumiko. But, most importantly, he knew that he had learned a very important lesson. He had learned that real courage means never taking the easy way out.